With my thanks to
San Kiu Lieu and Samantha Riches
who gave me the idea for this story and their
permission to use it when they were at
Keyworth Primary School in London.

American edition published in 2013 by Andersen Press USA,
an imprint of Andersen Press Ltd.
www.andersenpressusa.com
Paperback edition first published in 2009 by Andersen Press Ltd.
First published in Great Britain in 1999 by Andersen Press Ltd., 20 Vauxhall Bridge Road, London SW1V 2SA.
Published in Australia by Random House Australia Pty., Level 3, 100 Pacific Highway, North Sydney, NSW 2060.

Distributed in the United States and Canada by Lerner Publishing Group, Inc.
241 First Avenue North Minneapolis, MN 55401 U.S.A. www.lernerbooks.com
Color separated in Switzerland by Photolitho AG, Zürich.
Printed and bound in Malaysia by Tien Wah Press.
Library of Congress Cataloging-in-Publication Data Available.
ISBN: 978–1–4677–2047–2
ISBN: 978–1–4677–2048–9 (eBook)
1 – TWP – 3/27/13

tle Princess Story

I Want A Sister!

Tony Ross

Andersen Press USA

“There’s going to be someone new in our family,”
said the Queen.

"Oh goody!" said the Little Princess.
"We're going to get a dog."

“No we’re not,” said the King.
“We’re going to have a new baby.”

"Oh goody!" said the Little Princess.
"I want a sister."

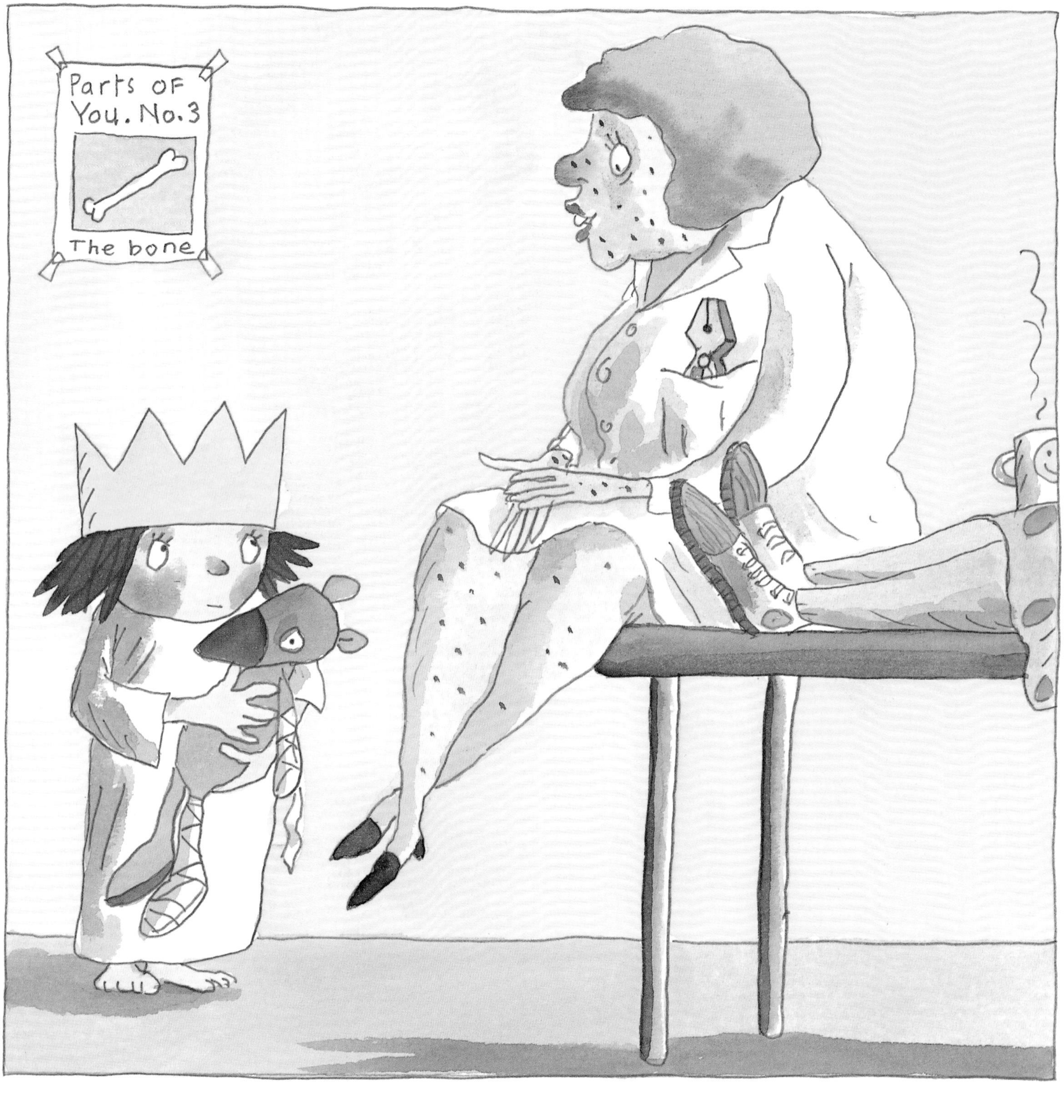

"It may be a brother," said the Doctor.
"You can't choose, you know."

“I don’t want a brother,” said the Little Princess.
“Brothers are smelly.”

“So are sisters,” said the Maid.
“Sometimes you smelled AWFUL.”

“I don’t want a brother,” said the Little Princess.
“Brothers are rough.”

"So are sisters," said the Admiral.
"Both make TERRIFIC sailors."

“I don’t want a brother,” said the Little Princess.
“Brothers have all the wrong toys.”

“Brothers’ toys can be just like yours,”
said the Prime Minister.

"Well," said the Little Princess,
"I JUST DON'T WANT A BROTHER."

“Why?” said everybody.
“BECAUSE I WANT A SISTER,” said the Little Princess.

One day, the Queen went to the hospital
to have the new baby.
"Don't forget . . ." shouted the Little Princess,

"... I WANT A SISTER!"

"What if it's a brother?" said her cousin.

"I'll put it in the trash," said the Little Princess.

When the Queen came home from hospital,
the King was carrying the new baby.

"Say 'hello' to the new baby," said the Queen.
"Isn't she lovely?" said the Little Princess.

“He isn’t a she,” said the King. “You have a brother.
A little Prince!”
“I don’t want a little Prince,” said the Little Princess.
“I want a little Princess.”

"But we already have a BEAUTIFUL little Princess,"
said the King and Queen.
"WHO?" said the Little Princess.

“YOU!” said the King and Queen.

"Can my brother have my potty? Now that I'm all grown up?"
said the Princess.

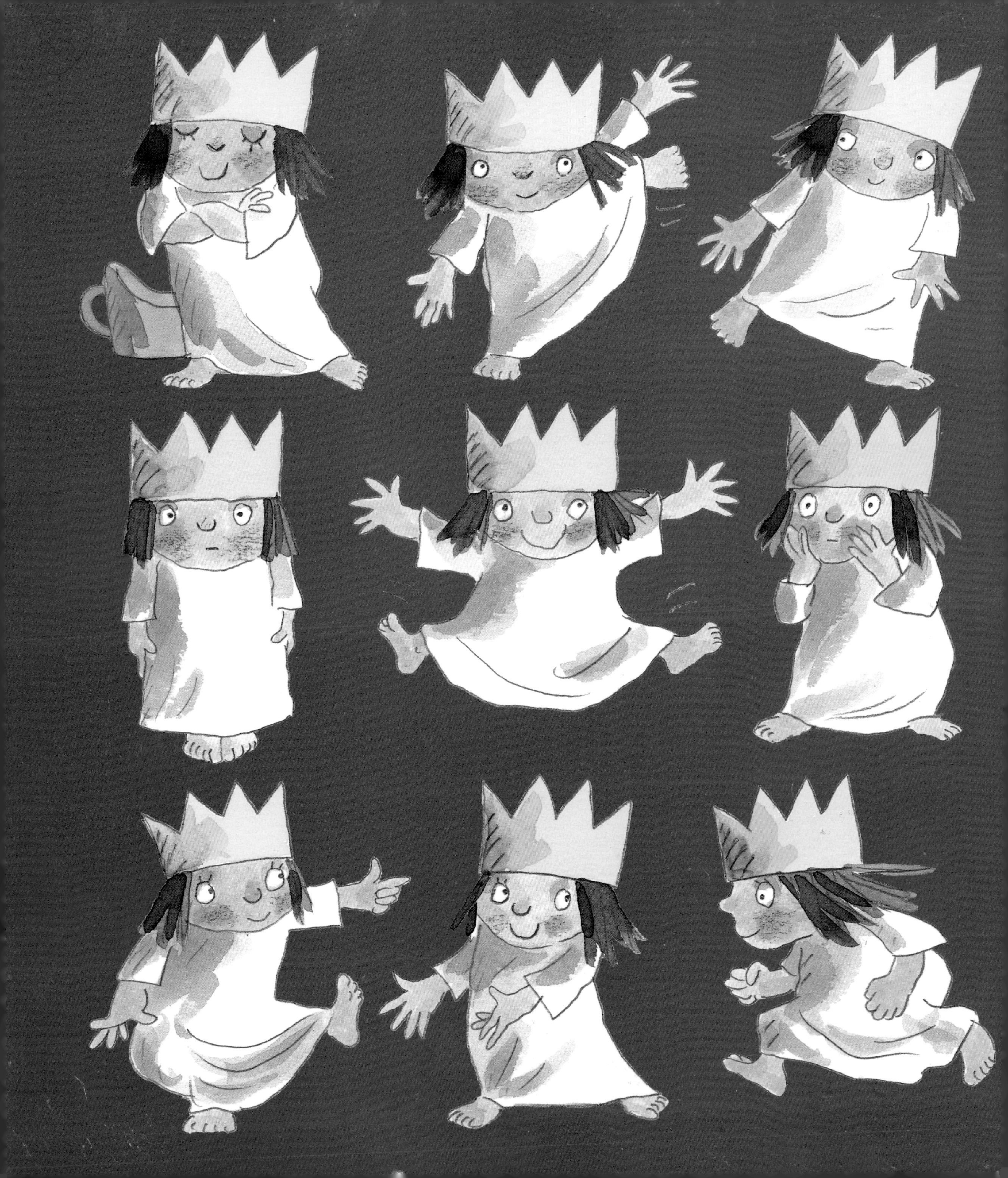